# Tillie and Mert

An I Can Read Book®

# Tillie and Mert
by Ida Luttrell
pictures by Doug Cushman

ABRIDGED EDITION

HarperCollins*Publishers*

Tillie and Mert
Text copyright © 1985 by Ida Luttrell
Illustrations copyright © 1985 by Doug Cushman
All rights reserved. No part of this book may be
used or reproduced in any manner whatsoever without
written permission except in the case of brief quotations
embodied in critical articles and reviews. Printed in
the United States of America. For information address
Harper & Row Junior Books, 10 East 53rd Street,
New York, N.Y. 10022.

Library of Congress Cataloging in Publication Data
Luttrell, Ida.
   Tillie and Mert.

   (An I can read book)
   Summary: Best friends Tillie and Mert do everything
together, from buying "bargains" at Weasel's garage sale
to telling fortunes and opening their own grocery store.
   I. Children's stories, American.  [1. Friendship—
Fiction.  2. Animals—Fiction]  I. Cushman, Doug, ill.
II. Title.  III. Series.
PZ7.L97953Ti 1985      [E]        85-42641
ISBN 0-06-024027-X
ISBN 0-06-024028-8 (lib. bdg.)

To my daughter, Anne
I.L.

For Jason
D.C.

# Contents

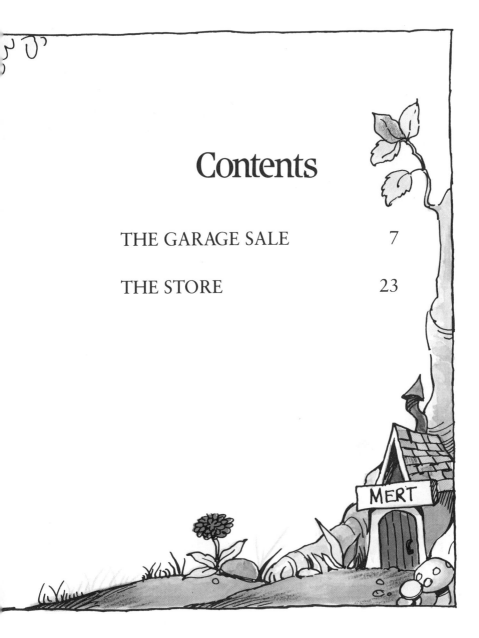

# The Garage Sale

Mert Fieldmouse was picking plums.

Tillie Skunk came running by.

"Mert," she cried,

"Weasel is having a garage sale.

Let's go."

"No, thanks," said Mert.

"I know all about Weasel's sales."

"But this is a good one,"

Tillie said.

She tugged at Mert's arm.

"Come on!"

Weasel was sitting by a table

covered with old things.

"Hello," said Weasel.

"I have lots of bargains for you."

Tillie picked up a pink umbrella.

"Just what I need," she said.

"Why are you selling this umbrella?"

"Well, it does have

a teeny tiny hole in it,"

said Weasel.

"But it would cost you

twice as much at the store."

"I want it," said Tillie.

She paid Weasel for the umbrella.

"What about this purse?" asked Mert.

"A fine purse," said Weasel.

"Real plastic. Hardly used at all."

"What is wrong with it?" asked Mert.

"Just a teeny tiny hole,"

said Weasel.

Mert put the purse back.

"I will take it," said Tillie.

She paid Weasel and put her change

in her new purse.

"Oh, look, Mert," said Tillie,

"I have always wanted a green teapot.

My old one is so plain."

"That is a real treasure,"

said Weasel.

"Is anything wrong with it?"

asked Tillie.

"Only a teeny tiny hole,"
said Weasel. "A new teapot
would be half as good."
"I will buy it," said Tillie.
Tillie paid Weasel for the teapot.
She was very pleased.
So was Weasel.
Tillie and Mert started home.

Suddenly it began to rain.

"We can use my new umbrella,"

said Tillie.

She opened the umbrella.

The rain came down harder.

The teeny tiny hole got larger.

Soon Mert and Tillie were very wet.

14

They ran to get out of the rain.

Tillie's money slipped

out the hole in her new purse.

"All my money is gone," she cried.

15

When they got to her house,

Tillie made some tea

in her new green teapot.

She set the teapot on the table.

A large brown stain

grew on her white tablecloth.

It grew bigger and bigger.

Tillie picked up the teapot.

All the tea was gone.

"Tillie," said Mert,

"we are cold and tired.

Your money is gone.

Your teapot won't hold tea.

Throw these bargains away."

"No," said Tillie,

and she thought very hard.

"I will plant a fern in the teapot.

I will use the umbrella for a hook.

I will hang my purse on the wall."

"What good is a purse

hanging on the wall?" asked Mert.

"It will remind me," said Tillie,

"never to buy a bargain

with a teeny tiny hole in it."

Mert laughed.

Then she and Tillie made tea

in Tillie's plain old teapot.

It was half the trouble

and twice as good.

# The Store

Tillie and Mert were eating pie.

"I have been thinking," said Tillie,

"about how we can get rich."

Mert stopped licking her fingers.

"How?" she asked.

"With a grocery store," said Tillie.

"Everyone eats."

"That sounds like fun," Mert said.

"Let's do it."

So Tillie and Mert

found just the right place

for the store.

They had many crates of groceries.

"I will put things on the shelves.

That is what I do best," said Mert.

"Good," Tillie said.

"I will work at the desk.

I am good at that."

Mert put baking powder

next to flea powder.

She put shampoo beside syrup,

and jelly beans beside lima beans.

Tillie's desk was piled with letters.

"Wonderful," she said.

"I love mail."

She opened a letter.

It said, "Pay your light bill."

"How boring," said Tillie.

She dropped the letter in the trash.

She opened another letter.

She read, "Your rent is due."

"Dull, dull, dull," Tillie said,

and she threw it away, too.

Pudge Gopher came into the store.

"Jelly beans, please," he said.

"These are better for you,"

Mert said.

She gave him a sack of lima beans.

28

Old Mr. Mole came in

to buy a can of baking powder.

He had left his glasses at home,

so he bought a can of flea powder.

Weasel rushed in.

"I am in a hurry," she said.

"Quick, where is your shampoo?"

"Over there," said Mert.

Weasel grabbed a bottle of syrup,

paid, and dashed out.

"But Weasel," called Mert.

Weasel was already gone.

The next morning

Mr. Mole came stomping in.

"Look at my biscuits!" he shouted.

"Your baking powder is no good."

Mert sniffed a biscuit.

"That smells like flea powder,"

she said.

"You should have read the label."

"I want my money back!" he yelled.

Just then Pudge came in.

"Your beans hurt my teeth," he said.

"Did you cook them?" asked Mert.

"No," he cried,

"I wanted jelly beans!"

Weasel stormed in.

"This terrible shampoo

ruined my hair!" she screamed.

"This is not bad shampoo,"

said Mert. "It is good syrup.

Take time when you shop."

Tillie came to see

what all the fuss was about.

"The customer is always right,"

she said.

She gave Mr. Mole

a fresh can of baking powder.

She gave

a sack of jelly beans to Pudge

and a bottle of shampoo to Weasel.

When they had all left, Tillie said,

"Mert, you are driving away

our customers."

Suddenly the lights went out.

"We must be having a storm,"

said Mert.

She and Tillie ran to the door.

The sun was shining.

"Did you pay the light bill?"

Mert cried.

"If you don't pay the light bill,

they turn off the lights."

"It was too boring," said Tillie.

Mert tripped over the trash can

in the dark store.

All the bills fell out.

"You don't know one thing

about desk work, Tillie," said Mert.

"We will have to close the store."

40

"Well," Tillie said, "you don't know

one thing about sorting groceries

or taking care of customers."

Now they were both angry.

"Could you do it better?"

Tillie and Mert shouted at once.

They looked at each other.

They started to laugh.

"Let's switch jobs," Tillie said.

So Mert paid the bills.

She counted the money

and took it to the bank.

Tillie sorted groceries

and helped the customers.

She always had jelly beans for Pudge.

Tillie and Mert

had the best store in town.

They did not make lots of money,

but they felt very rich.